ROWAN AVA SKYE

The Yeti's Arctic Christmas Adventure

Copyright © 2024 by Rowan Ava Skye

All rights reserved. No part of this publication may be reproduced, stored or transmitted in any form or by any means, electronic, mechanical, photocopying, recording, scanning, or otherwise without written permission from the publisher. It is illegal to copy this book, post it to a website, or distribute it by any other means without permission.

This novel is entirely a work of fiction. The names, characters and incidents portrayed in it are the work of the author's imagination. Any resemblance to actual persons, living or dead, events or localities is entirely coincidental.

First edition

ISBN: 9798301438981

This book was professionally typeset on Reedsy. Find out more at reedsy.com

Contents

Introduction	1
Chapter 1: The Glacier's Secret	3
Chapter 2: The Northern Lights' Whisper	6
Chapter 3: The Snow Owl's Prophecy	10
Chapter 4: The Frozen Timekeeper	14
Chapter 5: The Ice Giant's Trial	18
Chapter 6: A Christmas to Remember	22
Afterword	26

Introduction

The Arctic was silent, as it always was this time of year. The wind whispered across the snow-dusted tundra, carrying secrets only the frost and ice could understand. But tonight, the silence felt... heavier. The stars seemed dimmer, and the Northern Lights, usually a cascade of vibrant colors, flickered faintly as if holding back a message they dared not reveal.

Ty, a young yeti with a curious heart and an appetite for adventure, stood at the edge of a frozen cliff, staring at the sky. Something was wrong—he could feel it deep in his bones, an unsettling pull that made his fur stand on end. The Arctic didn't feel like home tonight.

"Ty, come back inside before you catch cold!" his mother called from their cozy den. But Ty didn't move. He couldn't.

There, in the distance, the lights twisted unnaturally, forming what looked like symbols—a language he didn't understand. His breath fogged in the icy air as he leaned forward, squinting at the strange shapes. Was it a warning? A call for help?

A sudden gust of wind howled past him, carrying with it something soft and delicate—a single snowflake, glowing faintly. Ty reached out instinctively, catching it in his hand. The snowflake shimmered for a moment before melting into a tiny puddle of water that formed... a map.

"What is this?" Ty whispered, his heart pounding. The map glowed faintly, pulsing as if alive, pointing him toward the farthest edge of the Arctic—the Glacier of Echoes, a place no one dared to venture.

Before he could decide what to do, the wind picked up again, this time carrying a faint, eerie sound. It wasn't just the howling of the storm—it was… laughter. Deep, chilling laughter that seemed to come from everywhere and nowhere all at once.

Ty's fur bristled. This wasn't just any Arctic night. Something—or someone—was calling him.

"Ty!" his mother called again, but this time her voice was tinged with fear.

Ty looked back toward the safety of his den, then down at the glowing map in his hand. He took a deep breath, his pulse racing.

Whatever was happening tonight, Ty knew one thing: it wasn't just about him. Something bigger was at stake—something far beyond his quiet Arctic life. And if the flickering lights and the mysterious map were any clue, this adventure would change Christmas forever.

But was Ty ready for the truth that awaited him in the frozen unknown?

As the wind howled again, Ty made his choice. The Arctic wouldn't stay silent for long.

Chapter 1: The Glacier's Secret

The Arctic wind howled as Yuletide—known to his friends (if he had any) as Ty—trudged through the endless white expanse. The mysterious letter in his hand shimmered faintly in the moonlight, its snowflake-like pattern shifting with every gust. The letter's cryptic message was clear:

"Find the Glacier that Glows. The answer to Christmas lies within."

Ty wasn't sure why the letter had found him. As a yeti, he had spent most of his life avoiding humans and their traditions. Christmas, with its bright lights and noisy cheer, had always seemed like a faraway dream—not something meant for someone like him. Yet here he was, miles from his warm cave, chasing a glowing glacier he wasn't even sure existed.

Just as doubt began to creep into his mind, Ty spotted something strange on the horizon. The moonlight caught a faint, shimmering light. It pulsed rhythmically, like a heartbeat, casting hues of blue and silver across the snow. Ty's heart raced. Was this the Glacier that Glows?

He hurried forward, the snow crunching beneath his massive feet. As he approached, the light grew brighter, revealing a towering wall of ice that seemed to breathe. Embedded in the glacier were veins of glowing, crystalline patterns that pulsed and shifted like living art.

Cautiously, Ty reached out and touched the ice. The moment his fingers brushed the cold surface, the patterns rearranged themselves, forming words:

"Speak the riddle, unlock the light."

A voice, soft and melodic, echoed around him. "Only those who seek with a true heart may enter."

Startled, Ty looked around. From behind the glacier stepped a creature unlike any he had ever seen. It was an arctic fox, but its fur shimmered with an ethereal glow, like moonlight trapped in a snowstorm. Its eyes, bright and intelligent, locked onto Ty.

"I'm Lumi," the fox said, its voice calm yet commanding. "You've come to the Glacier, but can you solve its secret?"

Ty frowned. "I didn't come here for riddles. I just… well, I…" He hesitated. Why *had* he come?

Lumi tilted her head, studying him. "The Glacier only reveals itself to those who need its magic. You've been chosen, Yeti. Now, the riddle:

"I am not alive, but I grow. I don't have lungs, but I need air. What am I?"

Ty scratched his head, the fur of his brow furrowing deeply. He wasn't much for riddles; his life had always been simple—find food, stay warm, avoid humans. But this wasn't just about him anymore. Something in Lumi's gaze told him that this was important.

"Not alive, but it grows…" Ty muttered. He glanced around, his eyes falling on the glacier's glowing patterns. The answer struck him like a gust of icy wind.

"It's ice," he said finally. "Ice isn't alive, but it grows. And it needs air to freeze."

The patterns on the glacier flared with a brilliant light, brighter than the northern stars. Lumi smiled. "You're smarter than you look, Yeti."

Before Ty could respond, the glacier began to shift. The ice creaked and groaned as a doorway appeared, leading into a cavern bathed in the same magical glow.

"Inside lies the key to saving Christmas," Lumi said, stepping into the cavern. "But beware—the answers you find may not be what you expect."

Ty followed, the cold air growing warmer as they descended. The walls sparkled with crystals, each reflecting a kaleidoscope of colors. At the center of the cavern was a pedestal, and on it rested a small, glowing orb.

Ty reached for the orb, but Lumi stopped him. "Careful," she warned. "This isn't just a gift—it's a choice."

"What do you mean?" Ty asked, confused.

CHAPTER 1: THE GLACIER'S SECRET

Lumi's glow dimmed slightly. "The orb holds a piece of Christmas magic, but it comes with a price. If you take it, you'll bind yourself to this journey. You'll be responsible for what comes next."

Ty hesitated. He had never asked to be part of this. But as he looked at the orb, he felt a warmth he hadn't known in years—a spark of belonging, of purpose.

"I'll do it," he said finally.

As his fingers closed around the orb, the cavern erupted with light. The walls shimmered, and the ice patterns danced like stars. But then, just as quickly as it began, the light vanished, leaving Ty holding the now-dark orb.

"What happened?" he asked, panic creeping into his voice.

Lumi's expression turned serious. "The magic has chosen you, but it's only the beginning. There's more to this journey than you realize, Ty. The Glacier's secret is not just the orb—it's you. You are part of the magic now."

Ty stared at the fox, his mind racing. What had he gotten himself into? And what did Lumi mean by *he* was part of the magic?

As they stepped out of the cavern, the Arctic wind seemed colder, sharper, as if the world itself had changed. The northern lights flickered in the sky, their colors shifting erratically.

"What now?" Ty asked.

Lumi's eyes glowed brighter. "Now, we find out what Christmas really needs saving from."

The chapter ends with Ty gripping the orb tightly, uncertainty swirling in his heart as the Arctic stretched out before him. What dangers lay ahead? And why did he feel like something—or someone—was watching them?

Chapter 2: The Northern Lights' Whisper

The Arctic night stretched endlessly around them, cold and quiet save for the crunch of Ty's heavy footsteps and Lumi's soft padding. Overhead, the Northern Lights danced with vibrant streaks of green, purple, and gold, their beauty mesmerizing even in the harsh cold. Ty couldn't shake the feeling, however, that something about them had changed.

"They've been moving like that for hours," he muttered, his voice breaking the silence. "Not just flowing like normal—more like they're… alive."

Lumi trotted ahead, her glowing tail flicking. "The Lights have always been more than they seem," she replied cryptically. "They hold secrets of the Arctic, whispers of what has been and what will be. Perhaps they've noticed us."

Ty shivered—not from the cold, but from Lumi's words. He craned his neck to look up again. This time, the Lights were forming something unmistakable: a swirling, spiral shape that tightened and loosened like a heartbeat.

"Are they guiding us or trying to scare us off?" Ty asked.

Lumi paused, her sharp ears twitching. "It's hard to say. The Lights don't speak directly, but their warnings are never without reason." She glanced at Ty, her glowing eyes narrowing. "We'd better keep moving."

As they pressed on, the landscape began to change. The open tundra gave way to a dense ice forest, the crystalline trees glittering like frozen chandeliers under the light of the auroras. The ground crunched louder beneath Ty's feet, the sound echoing unnaturally.

"Why is it so loud?" Ty whispered, his voice uneasy.

Lumi sniffed the air and froze. "It's not just your footsteps," she said, her fur bristling. "Something's listening."

CHAPTER 2: THE NORTHERN LIGHTS' WHISPER

Ty whipped around, scanning the forest, but saw nothing. The trees stood motionless, their icy branches swaying faintly in the wind. Yet the echoes continued, growing sharper and closer with every step.

"We need to hurry," Lumi urged, her glowing form darting ahead.

Ty tried to keep up, but the forest seemed to close in around him. The trees leaned inward, their icy branches weaving together to form an almost maze-like path. The Northern Lights above dimmed, their vibrant colors fading to a pale blue, casting eerie shadows on the snow.

"Lumi?" Ty called out, his deep voice trembling slightly.

"I'm here," came the fox's reply, though her voice sounded farther away than before. "Just follow the echoes—but be careful. They're trying to trick you."

Ty stumbled forward, each step ringing out like a bell. He felt as though the sound was bouncing back at him, distorting, growing louder and louder until it was nearly unbearable. He clutched the dark orb in his hand, hoping its strange magic might offer some protection, but it remained cold and inert.

Suddenly, the path split in three directions, each one framed by glistening ice arches. Ty stopped, his breath visible in the freezing air.

"Lumi?" he called again, but this time, there was no response.

Instead, the echoes changed. They were no longer his footsteps—they were voices. Whispered, indistinct, but undeniably voices.

"Ty..."

He spun around, his heart racing. The voices were coming from the middle path, soft but insistent.

"Come this way, Ty..."

On instinct, Ty stepped back, his claws crunching in the snow. Something about the voices felt wrong, like they were wrapping around his thoughts, pulling him forward against his will. He squeezed the orb tighter.

"No," he muttered to himself, forcing his legs to stay still. "This is a trick."

As if in response, the Northern Lights flickered violently above him. The voices grew louder, more desperate. Ty shut his eyes, trying to block them out, when he heard Lumi's voice cutting through the noise.

"Ty, don't move!"

His eyes snapped open. Lumi stood at the far end of the left path, her fur glowing brighter than ever. "That middle path—it's a trap! Hurry, this way!"

Without hesitation, Ty bolted toward her. As he passed the middle path, the ice arches shattered with a deafening crack, and a swirling vortex of black snow erupted from within. The voices turned into an eerie wail, and the vortex reached out like icy fingers, narrowly missing Ty as he leapt to safety.

Panting, Ty landed beside Lumi, who was staring at the now-sealed path with a grim expression.

"What… what was that?" Ty gasped, his breath fogging the air.

"The forest doesn't want us here," Lumi said, her voice low. "It's testing us, trying to turn us back. But we can't stop now."

As they continued down the left path, the echoes finally faded, replaced by an unsettling silence. The trees thinned, and the forest opened into a clearing. At its center stood an enormous frozen pillar, its surface smooth and reflective like a mirror.

The Northern Lights above twisted again, forming another shape—a key.

Ty stepped closer to the pillar, his reflection staring back at him. But as he moved, his reflection didn't follow. Instead, it smiled—a slow, knowing grin that sent a chill down Ty's spine.

"That's not me," Ty whispered.

"No," Lumi said, her voice barely audible. "That's the Guardian of the Forest."

The reflection raised a hand, pressing it against the ice. Ty hesitated, then mirrored the gesture. The moment his palm touched the pillar, a crack split through the ice, and the reflection vanished.

The ground shook, and the pillar dissolved into a shower of glittering snowflakes, revealing a small, intricately carved key suspended in midair.

Ty grabbed it, the cold metal biting into his hand.

"This key," he said, turning to Lumi, "what does it open?"

Lumi's eyes glowed brighter, her expression unreadable. "That depends," she said softly. "On whether you're ready to face the next truth."

The chapter ends with the forest behind them rumbling ominously, as if the echoes hadn't disappeared but merely been waiting. Ty tightened his grip

CHAPTER 2: THE NORTHERN LIGHTS' WHISPER

on the key, knowing this was only the beginning of the dangers ahead.

Chapter 3: The Snow Owl's Prophecy

The Arctic wilderness grew even more desolate as Ty and Lumi ventured further, the horizon a pale blur against the endless stretch of white. Ty's breath fogged in front of him, and the key he'd retrieved from the ice pillar felt heavy in his pocket, its strange carvings etched deeply into his mind.

"What now?" Ty asked, breaking the silence. "We've got the key, but no idea what it opens or where to go."

Lumi stopped suddenly, her glowing fur shimmering faintly in the dim light. "We wait," she said.

"For what?"

"For him," she replied cryptically, her ears twitching.

Before Ty could ask what she meant, a sudden gust of wind swept through the tundra, carrying with it a sound—a haunting, echoing cry that sent shivers down his spine. Ty looked up, shielding his eyes against the wind, and saw a massive figure descending from the swirling clouds above.

It was a snow owl, its feathers gleaming like frost and its wingspan so large it seemed to blot out the sky. The bird landed gracefully in front of them, its sharp, golden eyes locking onto Ty with an intensity that made him freeze.

"Tyson, son of the Arctic winds," the owl spoke, its deep voice resonating like the hum of a glacier. "I have been waiting for you."

"You… you know my name?" Ty stammered.

The owl nodded solemnly. "I am Orlin, Keeper of the Northern Prophecy. Your arrival was foretold long before the first snow fell this winter."

Lumi bowed her head. "Orlin, it's an honor," she said.

CHAPTER 3: THE SNOW OWL'S PROPHECY

Ty, still stunned, struggled to find words. "Prophecy? What prophecy?"

Orlin flapped his great wings, sending a cascade of snow swirling around them. "The prophecy of the Guardian of Christmas," he intoned. "It is said that one with the heart of a protector and the courage of a wanderer would rise to defend the season of giving when it is most threatened."

Ty frowned. "I think you've got the wrong guy. I'm just trying to figure out what's going on."

The owl's golden eyes narrowed. "You carry the key, do you not?"

Ty hesitated, then pulled the key from his pocket, holding it up. The carvings glinted in the faint light, and Orlin's gaze softened.

"That key," the owl said, "is one part of the prophecy. But the path ahead remains incomplete. The prophecy is missing a piece—a choice must be made to unlock its full power."

"What kind of choice?" Ty asked cautiously.

Orlin gestured with one great wing toward the horizon. "At the edge of the Arctic abyss lies the answer. But beware: the choice is not without cost."

Ty exchanged a nervous glance with Lumi. "What happens if I make the wrong choice?"

"The prophecy unravels," Orlin said grimly. "And with it, so does the hope of saving Christmas."

Ty's stomach churned, but he clenched his fists. "Then I guess we'd better find this abyss."

The owl nodded. "Follow the lights," he said, gesturing toward the sky. "They will guide you. But tread carefully—there are those who would seek to twist the prophecy for their own ends."

With a mighty beat of his wings, Orlin lifted into the air, disappearing into the clouds as suddenly as he'd appeared.

As they followed the faint glow of the Northern Lights, the terrain grew more treacherous. The snow deepened, and jagged ice formations jutted out of the ground like frozen teeth. Lumi's glow was the only thing keeping Ty grounded as the wind howled around them.

Finally, they reached the edge of the abyss. It was a gaping chasm, its depths shrouded in shadow. A narrow ice bridge stretched across it, barely wide enough for one person to cross.

"What now?" Ty asked, staring into the void.

Lumi sniffed the air, her glowing eyes scanning the surroundings. "The choice lies across the bridge," she said. "But crossing won't be easy."

As if in answer, the wind picked up, and a deep rumble echoed from the abyss. Ty felt the ground beneath his feet tremble and looked down to see cracks forming in the ice.

"We have to move," Lumi urged.

Ty stepped onto the bridge, his claws scraping against the slippery surface. Each step felt like a gamble, the ice creaking ominously beneath his weight. Lumi followed closely, her glow reflecting off the icy walls.

Halfway across, a chilling voice rose from the depths of the abyss.

"Turn back," it whispered, low and haunting. "The choice is not yours to make."

Ty froze. The voice was everywhere and nowhere, filling the air around them. Lumi growled, her fur bristling.

"Keep going," she said, her voice firm. "Don't listen to it."

But the voice grew louder, more insistent. "The key will betray you," it hissed. "The Guardian is a lie."

Ty's heart pounded, doubt creeping into his mind. He looked down at the key in his hand, its carvings suddenly unfamiliar and foreboding.

"Ty!" Lumi's sharp bark snapped him out of it. "Don't stop!"

He took another step, then another, until they finally reached the other side. The moment they stepped off the bridge, the ice behind them shattered, pieces tumbling into the abyss with a deafening crash.

Breathing heavily, Ty turned to Lumi. "What was that voice?"

"Something old," she said, her eyes narrowing. "Something that doesn't want the prophecy fulfilled."

Ahead of them stood a pedestal carved from ice, its surface etched with strange symbols. At its center was a hollow, perfectly shaped to fit the key.

Ty hesitated, the weight of Orlin's words heavy on his mind. This was the choice. But what if the voice had been right?

He glanced at Lumi, who nodded encouragingly. "Trust yourself," she said.

CHAPTER 3: THE SNOW OWL'S PROPHECY

Taking a deep breath, Ty placed the key into the hollow. For a moment, nothing happened. Then the ground shook violently, and a blinding light erupted from the pedestal.

When the light faded, the abyss was gone, replaced by a shimmering pathway of ice stretching into the horizon. But Ty's relief was short-lived—at the end of the path stood a shadowy figure, its form indistinct but its intent unmistakably hostile.

Lumi growled low in her throat. "The prophecy wasn't just about finding the key," she said. "It's about proving you're worthy to wield it."

Ty clenched his fists, determination hardening in his chest. "Then let's prove it."

The chapter ends with the shadow stepping forward, its icy footsteps echoing ominously as Ty and Lumi prepare to face their next challenge.

Chapter 4: The Frozen Timekeeper

The shimmering ice path led Ty and Lumi through an otherworldly landscape, where the sky glowed faintly with swirling auroras. It was as if the Northern Lights themselves were alive, guiding them toward a mysterious destination. In the distance, a shadowy silhouette emerged—a towering structure encased in layers of glittering ice.

As they approached, Ty's breath caught in his throat. "Is that… a clock tower?"

The structure loomed like a frozen giant, its spire reaching toward the heavens. Every inch was covered in intricate frost patterns that shimmered with an otherworldly light. The clock face was cracked and dark, its hands frozen at midnight. At its base, a massive iron door was barely visible beneath the encasing ice.

"This has to be it," Lumi murmured, her glow intensifying as she stepped closer. "The Frozen Timekeeper."

"Timekeeper?" Ty asked.

"It's said to control the flow of time in the Arctic," Lumi explained. "If it stops, so does the magic of this land."

Ty felt a shiver run down his spine—not from the cold, but from the weight of what Lumi had said. He reached out to touch the frozen door, and as his claws scraped against the ice, the tower seemed to groan, a low, eerie sound that echoed through the air.

Suddenly, the ice began to crack. Lumi jumped back, her fur bristling. Ty stumbled as the ground beneath them trembled.

The cracks spread across the tower's surface, and with a deafening crash,

CHAPTER 4: THE FROZEN TIMEKEEPER

the ice shattered. The door creaked open, revealing a dimly lit interior.

"Guess we're going in," Ty said, trying to steady his nerves.

Inside, the air was eerily still. The walls were lined with gears and cogs, all frozen in place. A massive pendulum hung in the center, its surface frosted over. The floor was a mosaic of timepieces, their hands stopped at different hours.

"This place is ancient," Lumi said, her voice barely a whisper. "And it's broken. We have to fix it."

"Fix it how?" Ty asked, staring at the complex machinery.

Lumi pointed to the top of the tower. "The core is up there. If we restart it, the Timekeeper should begin working again. But we'll have to be careful—this place is tied to time itself. If something goes wrong…"

She didn't need to finish the sentence. Ty nodded, swallowing his fear.

They began climbing a spiral staircase that wound around the tower's interior. With every step, the air grew colder, and Ty's breath turned to frost. As they neared the top, the clock face came into view, its shattered glass casting jagged reflections.

At the center of the tower was the core—a glowing orb suspended in a network of frozen gears. It pulsed faintly, as if alive, but its light was flickering.

"This is it," Lumi said. "We need to turn it back on."

"How?" Ty asked, eyeing the intricate machinery.

Lumi's ears twitched. "The key," she said.

Ty pulled the key from his pocket, its carvings glowing faintly in response to the orb's light. He hesitated, then stepped forward and placed the key into a slot at the base of the core.

The moment the key clicked into place, the tower shuddered. The gears groaned, and the pendulum twitched. The orb's light grew brighter, and for a moment, Ty thought they had succeeded.

But then, everything went wrong.

The tower erupted in a cascade of light and sound. Ty and Lumi were thrown backward as the core pulsed violently. The walls shimmered, and suddenly, the room around them began to change.

Images appeared in the air—ghostly, translucent scenes that swirled like snowflakes. Ty recognized the first scene immediately: a warm Christmas morning from his childhood, with his family laughing around a crackling fire. He felt a pang of nostalgia, but before he could reach out, the image shifted.

Now he saw Lumi, alone in a snow-covered forest. She was smaller, younger, her fur dimmer. She was searching for something, her eyes filled with sadness.

"Lumi?" Ty said, turning to her.

Lumi's ears flattened. "It's the past," she whispered. "The Timekeeper is unraveling time itself."

Before Ty could respond, the scene changed again. This time, it showed a bustling Christmas market filled with joy and light. But as they watched, the colors began to fade, the people vanishing one by one until only an empty, snow-covered street remained.

"What's happening?" Ty asked, his voice trembling.

"This is the present," Lumi said, her glow dimming. "The magic of Christmas is disappearing."

The images shifted once more, and this time, Ty's blood ran cold. The scene was dark, desolate. The Arctic was a wasteland, its ice blackened and broken. The clock tower was in ruins, its pieces scattered across the tundra.

"This… this can't be real," Ty said, his voice barely audible.

"It's the future," Lumi said, her voice heavy with dread. "The one we have to stop."

The core pulsed again, and the images vanished. The tower grew still, the silence deafening.

"We have to fix this," Ty said, his fists clenched. "Before it's too late."

Lumi nodded, her determination returning. "The Timekeeper is trying to show us what's at stake. But it's not over yet."

They approached the core once more, and Lumi placed her paw on the glowing surface. "We need to align the gears," she said. "And fast."

Together, they worked to unfreeze the machinery. Ty used his claws to scrape away the frost while Lumi's glow melted the ice. Slowly, the gears began to turn. The pendulum started to swing, its motion steady and rhythmic.

CHAPTER 4: THE FROZEN TIMEKEEPER

As the core's light stabilized, the tower seemed to breathe again. The clock face repaired itself, and the hands began to move. The images did not return, but Ty felt a strange sense of hope.

But just as they were about to celebrate, the tower shook violently. A crack appeared in the floor, spreading toward the core.

"What's happening?" Ty shouted.

Lumi's eyes widened. "The Timekeeper isn't fully stable. Something—or someone—is interfering."

Before Ty could react, a figure emerged from the shadows. It was cloaked in ice, its face obscured, and its voice was cold and sharp.

"You think you can control time?" the figure said, its tone mocking. "Time does not belong to you."

Ty stepped in front of Lumi, his claws unsheathed. "Who are you?"

The figure laughed, a sound like shattering ice. "I am the Warden of Frost," it said. "And you are trespassing in my domain."

The chapter ends with the Warden raising its icy staff, the tower plunging into chaos as Ty and Lumi prepare to face their greatest challenge yet.

Chapter 5: The Ice Giant's Trial

The ground beneath Ty's feet gave way, sending him plummeting into a cavern so deep that the light of the auroras above faded into darkness. Lumi's glow, faint but steady, illuminated jagged walls of ice surrounding them. Each surface reflected their worried faces in distorted, ghostly forms.

"Where are we?" Ty asked, his voice trembling.

"The Heart of the Deep," Lumi replied, her glow flickering. "This is where the Ice Giant dwells. It's said no one leaves without facing the truth of who they are."

Before Ty could respond, a rumble echoed through the cavern, shaking the icy walls. Lumi's ears perked up, and she pressed closer to Ty. The rumble grew louder until it became a deafening roar.

Suddenly, a massive figure emerged from the shadows. The Ice Giant was colossal, its crystalline form shimmering with an otherworldly light. Its eyes glowed like twin glaciers, ancient and knowing, as it loomed over them.

"Who dares enter my domain?" the giant bellowed, its voice reverberating like thunder.

Ty stepped forward, his legs trembling. "I'm Ty, and this is Lumi. We're here to save Christmas."

The Ice Giant tilted its head, studying him. "Save Christmas?" it repeated, a hint of amusement in its voice. "Do you think yourself worthy of such a task?"

Ty swallowed hard but nodded. "I have to try."

The giant's laughter boomed through the cavern, shaking loose shards of

CHAPTER 5: THE ICE GIANT'S TRIAL

ice that crashed to the ground. "Then you must face my trial," it said. "Only those with courage and a pure heart can succeed. But be warned—this test will reveal your deepest fears and challenge the truth of your intentions."

Before Ty could protest, the Ice Giant slammed its massive hands together. The cavern dissolved around them, and Ty suddenly found himself in a snowy meadow under a pale, gray sky. Lumi was nowhere to be seen.

"Lumi?" Ty called, his voice echoing in the empty air.

A soft wind stirred the snow, and whispers filled the air. Ty turned, and his heart sank. In the distance, he saw his family standing together, their forms hazy like mirages. He tried to run toward them, but no matter how fast he moved, they stayed just out of reach.

"Why did you leave us, Ty?" his mother's voice called, laced with sorrow.

Ty froze. "I didn't leave—I'm trying to help!" he shouted, his voice cracking.

The whispers grew louder, and the mirages faded, replaced by towering shadows that loomed over him. Each shadow resembled a fear he couldn't ignore—failure, loneliness, and doubt.

"You can't save anyone," the shadows hissed. "You're just a scared little yeti pretending to be brave."

Ty clenched his fists, his breath coming in shallow gasps. The weight of their words pressed down on him, threatening to crush his resolve.

Then, faintly, he heard another voice—a familiar one.

"Ty, don't listen to them!" Lumi's voice echoed, cutting through the darkness.

He looked up and saw a faint glow in the distance. Lumi's form appeared, her eyes bright with determination.

"You've already come this far," she said. "Don't let fear stop you now!"

Ty took a deep breath and forced himself to move forward. The shadows clawed at him, their whispers growing more desperate, but he focused on Lumi's voice and the faint warmth it brought. Step by step, he pushed through the darkness until the shadows began to fade.

The snowy meadow dissolved, and Ty found himself back in the cavern. Lumi stood beside him, her glow stronger than before. The Ice Giant watched from above, its expression unreadable.

"You faced your fears," the giant rumbled. "But the trial is not over."

Before Ty could ask what it meant, the ground split open, revealing a massive chasm filled with swirling light. The giant gestured to the abyss.

"Courage alone is not enough," it said. "Kindness must guide your actions. Leap into the chasm, and prove your heart's intent."

Ty stared at the swirling void, his stomach twisting in knots. "What's at the bottom?"

"The unknown," the giant replied. "You must trust yourself—and your companion—to find the truth."

Ty hesitated, his feet rooted to the ground. What if it was a trap? What if he failed?

Lumi nudged his leg gently. "You've come this far, Ty. I believe in you."

Her words filled him with a strange, quiet confidence. Taking a deep breath, he stepped to the edge. "Here goes nothing," he whispered, then leaped into the void.

The sensation was unlike anything Ty had ever felt. He was weightless, spinning through a kaleidoscope of light and color. Memories swirled around him—his happiest moments, his greatest regrets, and fleeting glimpses of a future he didn't yet understand.

Through it all, a warm light grew brighter, pulling him forward.

When he finally landed, the world around him was different. He stood in a radiant chamber made entirely of shimmering ice. At its center was a glowing crystal shaped like a snowflake, pulsing with a gentle, rhythmic light.

"The Heart of Christmas Magic," Lumi whispered, her voice filled with awe.

The Ice Giant's voice echoed through the chamber. "You have proven yourself, Ty. Courage brought you here, but kindness lights the way forward. Take the Heart, and restore the magic of this land."

Ty hesitated, then reached out to touch the crystal. The moment his fingers brushed its surface, a surge of warmth spread through him. The light from the crystal grew, filling the chamber and then spilling out into the cavern beyond.

When the light faded, Ty found himself back on solid ground, Lumi by his side. The Ice Giant knelt before them, its massive form now glowing softly.

CHAPTER 5: THE ICE GIANT'S TRIAL

"You have succeeded," it said, its voice reverent. "But your journey is not yet complete. The magic is restored, but the Warden of Frost will not give up so easily. Prepare yourself, Guardian of Christmas."

Ty's eyes widened. "Guardian of Christmas?"

The Ice Giant nodded. "The title is yours, but the responsibility is great. Go now, and finish what you have started."

As Ty and Lumi stepped away from the Ice Giant, the weight of their task settled over him. But for the first time, Ty felt something else—a quiet, unshakable hope.

The chapter ends with Ty and Lumi climbing out of the cavern, their next challenge looming just beyond the horizon.

Chapter 6: A Christmas to Remember

Ty emerged from the Ice Giant's cavern, the Heart of Christmas Magic glowing softly in his hands. The cold wind of the Arctic greeted him like an old friend, but the sky above was not the same. What had once been painted with the soft hues of the Northern Lights now churned with dark clouds and streaks of ominous red.

"Something's wrong," Lumi whispered, her glowing fur dimming slightly.

Ty nodded, clutching the Heart tighter. He could feel its warmth pulsing against his chest like a quiet reminder to keep going. But the journey back wasn't going to be easy—not with the sky rumbling like an oncoming storm.

As they trudged through the snow, a shadow appeared on the horizon. It moved swiftly, growing larger until Ty could make out a towering figure draped in icy armor—the Warden of Frost.

"I told you this would end in failure," the Warden bellowed, his voice like shattering glaciers. "You think you can save Christmas with a glowing trinket?"

Ty stepped forward, his knees shaking but his resolve firm. "It's not just a trinket," he said. "It's the Heart of Christmas, and it's more powerful than your fear."

The Warden laughed, a sound that made the ground quake. "You've learned nothing. Magic is fleeting, boy. Fear is eternal."

The Warden raised his icy staff, and the storm around them intensified. Snow swirled into a blinding blizzard, and the air grew so cold that Ty's breath froze in front of him.

In the chaos, Lumi jumped in front of Ty. "You have the Heart! Use it!"

CHAPTER 6: A CHRISTMAS TO REMEMBER

Ty hesitated. The Heart pulsed gently in his hands, as if waiting for him to act. But what was he supposed to do? He wasn't some magical hero—he was just Ty, a yeti trying to help.

"Do you truly think you're the Guardian of Christmas?" the Warden sneered. "You're nothing but a scared child who got lucky."

Ty's grip on the Heart tightened. The Warden's words cut deep, but as he glanced down at Lumi, he saw her unwavering faith in him. And then he remembered the Ice Giant's words: *Kindness lights the way forward.*

Closing his eyes, Ty focused on the warmth of the Heart. He thought of his family waiting for him, of the joy he felt when he saw the Northern Lights for the first time, and of the kindness he had experienced from Lumi and Orlin.

"Christmas isn't about fear," Ty said, his voice steady despite the storm. "It's about connection, bravery, and hope. And that's stronger than anything you can throw at me."

The Heart began to glow brighter, its warmth spreading through the icy landscape. The blizzard slowed, the snowflakes shimmering like tiny stars as they drifted to the ground. The Warden staggered back, shielding his eyes from the brilliant light.

"No!" the Warden roared. "This can't be!"

Ty stepped forward, holding the Heart high. The light grew until it enveloped the Warden completely. For a moment, Ty thought the Warden would lash out, but instead, the icy armor around him cracked and shattered.

When the light faded, the Warden was gone. In his place stood a small, frail figure—a boy no older than Ty, with sad eyes and frostbitten cheeks.

"What... what happened to me?" the boy asked, his voice trembling.

"You were trapped by fear," Lumi said softly. "But the Heart of Christmas has freed you."

The boy looked at Ty, tears welling in his eyes. "I didn't mean to hurt anyone. I just... I was so alone."

Ty knelt beside him and placed a comforting hand on his shoulder. "You don't have to be alone anymore. Christmas is about coming together, no matter how lost you feel."

The storm cleared, revealing a breathtaking sky painted with vibrant colors.

The Northern Lights danced joyfully, and the Heart of Christmas Magic glowed brighter than ever. Ty felt a surge of pride and relief, but he knew his journey wasn't over yet.

"We need to get back," Ty said, glancing at Lumi. "Christmas is waiting."

With the boy—the former Warden—following close behind, Ty and Lumi raced across the Arctic. The Heart's glow seemed to guide their way, illuminating hidden paths and melting obstacles in their path.

As they approached the small Arctic village where Ty's family lived, the Heart began to hum softly, its light spreading outward like ripples in water.

Ty entered the village square, where a group of yetis and animals had gathered in the dim light of dawn. His family was among them, their worried faces lighting up when they saw him.

"Ty!" his mother cried, rushing forward to hug him.

"You did it!" his father said, beaming with pride.

Ty held up the Heart, its glow now filling the entire village. "I didn't do it alone," he said, glancing at Lumi and the boy. "But we saved Christmas."

The Heart's light spread to every corner of the village, igniting lanterns, decorating trees with sparkling frost, and filling the air with a warmth that felt like pure joy.

The boy stepped forward, looking at the villagers with wide eyes. "I'm so sorry for what I've done," he said. "I was lost for so long… but Ty showed me the way back."

The villagers surrounded him, their expressions kind and forgiving.

"Christmas is about second chances," Ty said, smiling.

As the first rays of sunlight broke over the horizon, the village erupted in celebration. Ty's family embraced him, Lumi danced playfully around the Heart, and the boy—now free of his icy curse—laughed for the first time in years.

But as the festivities continued, Ty felt a strange tug in his chest. The Heart of Christmas Magic pulsed gently, as if speaking to him.

"What's wrong?" Lumi asked, noticing his thoughtful expression.

"I think this is just the beginning," Ty said, his eyes on the horizon. "There's more out there—more people who need the magic of Christmas."

CHAPTER 6: A CHRISTMAS TO REMEMBER

Lumi's eyes sparkled. "Then let's go find them."

With the Heart of Christmas Magic in hand and Lumi by his side, Ty knew his adventure wasn't over. But for now, he would cherish this Christmas—a Christmas to remember, not because of the magic but because of the connections he had made along the way.

And as the Northern Lights danced above, Ty couldn't help but feel that the best was yet to come.

Afterword

Dear Readers,

Thank you for joining Ty and Lumi on their incredible journey through the Arctic in *The Yeti's Arctic Christmas Adventure*. I hope their story filled your heart with wonder, bravery, and the magic of connection. Every step Ty took reminded us all that the true magic of Christmas lies in kindness, courage, and the love we share with those around us.

This adventure may have come to an end, but Ty's story is just the beginning! Keep an eye out in the coming days for more tales from the Arctic and beyond—stories filled with wonder, twists, and heartwarming lessons for every season.

Don't forget to explore our series for other magical adventures featuring your favorite holidays and celebrations! Each story is perfect for sharing with family, gifting to friends, or curling up with on a cozy evening.

From all of us here, thank you for reading, and may your days be filled with joy, magic, and endless adventures!

Warm wishes and happy reading,

P.S. Don't forget to check out our upcoming books! Whether it's a tropical Christmas adventure, a spooky Halloween tale, or a love-filled Valentine's journey, there's always something magical waiting just for you. Stay tuned!

Made in United States
Cleveland, OH
03 December 2024